GHOST IN THE HOUSE

GHOST IN THE

HOUSE

Ammi-Joan Paquette

illustrated by
Adam Record

CANDLEWICK PRESS

BOO!

There's a ghost in the house,
In the creepy haunted house,
On this dark, spooky night, all alone.

And he goes slip-slide
With a swoop and a glide
Until suddenly he hears . . .

A GROAN!

And a mummy makes two in the house,

In the creepy haunted house,

On this dark, spooky night, on the prowl.

And they shuffle around
Without even a sound
Until suddenly they hear . . .

A GROWL!

And a monster makes three in the house,
In the creepy haunted house,
On this dark, spooky night, midnight black.

And they creep and crawl
Down the echoing hall
Until suddenly they hear . . .

CLICK-
CLACK!

And a skeleton makes four in the house,
In the creepy haunted house,
On this dark, spooky night, cold and bleak.

And they stagger and stomp
In a spine-chilling romp
Until suddenly they hear . . .

A SHRIEK!

And a witch makes five in the house,
In the creepy haunted house,
On this dark, spooky night — best beware!

Then a sudden FLASH
Makes them topple and crash,
And suddenly they hear . . .

There's a boy in the house,

In the creepy haunted house,

On this dark, spooky night — what a fright!

ive, four, three, two, one —

ll the creatures run!

eaving him alone to say . . .

"GOOD NIGHT?!"

For Lils,
in memory of those long-ago days
of "the Es and the As"
A. J. P.

To my kids, Haven and Liam
A. R.

First paperback edition 2019

Library of Congress Catalog Card Number 2012943659
ISBN 978-0-7636-5529-7 (hardcover)
ISBN 978-0-7636-7622-3 (lift-the-flap edition)
ISBN 978-0-7636-9892-8 (paperback)

19 20 21 22 23 24 APS 10 9 8 7 6 5 4 3 2 1

Printed in Humen, Dongguan, China

This book was typeset in Historical Fell Type Roman and Carrotflower.
The illustrations were created digitally.

Candlewick Press
99 Dover Street
Somerville, Massachusetts 02144

visit us at www.candlewick.com